Awakings

Book 1 of The Taslasness Chronicles

Awakings

Book 1 of The Taslasness Chronicles

Kevin James Keyser

Kevin James Keyser

2015

Second Printing: February 2015
ISBN 978-0-578-15706-1
Kevin James Keyser
www.kevin-keyser.com

Acknowledgements

I would like to thank the following people for their help and support:

- Aura Pocklington – Editor and Proofreader
- Taly Reznik – Cover Art

Introduction

This is the first in a series of stories already told. "Huh" you say? Let me explain;

In 1974 the entertainment group I headed produced the following story as an audio play. An audio play is a modern take on a radio play. It's a dramatization on tape.

The original audio play was meant to be a one shot plot device to introduce a new character to the series.

It's funny; the original series has been long forgotten, but the one shot plot device is still with us!

Over the years I have written at least 5 stories based on the first one, with many more in outline form.

Yet very few readers know of <u>this</u> story because it was an audio play. Since this story **is** the Genesis for the series I decided to re-write it in story format.

Eventually I will combine all these stories in to one "Taslasness Mega Tome". Until then please enjoy reading "Awakings"!

Kevin

James

Keyser

Of Wizards and Granddaughters

She runs in to the room, almost shaking the pots of herbs off the shelf.

"Grandfather!"

The old man jumps and almost drops what looks to be a floundering fish, except each movement generates notes in a song, a song that seems to come from nowhere and everywhere.

He puts the "fish" in to a large wooden barrel and covers it with an equally large wooden top.

"What is it child?!"

"Hey! I'm no child, I'm 16!"

"Cassiopeia, when you get as old as me almost *anyone* is considered a child!"

"Well I just thought you'd be interested, that's all."

"Interested in what?"

"I just did it!"

"You did it?

"Yeah!"

"You did it; <u>what</u>?"

"Watch!"

She holds out her right hand, reaches out towards a beam of sunlight coming through the window and nothing happens.

"Oh, <u>that's</u> what you are talking about."

"Awww, it worked before!"

"You are trying too hard; don't try just know that you can do it."

"Yes, Yoda!"

"Yoda?"

"Never mind!"

"Where do you want to go?"

"The river, I want to hear some new songs."

"Just picture the river in your head, feel it, hear its bubbling water."

"I see it."

"Grab the light beam, child."

She reaches out again; her hand touches the sunlight and begins to move into it, *blurring* and becoming longer. She laughs as her whole body becomes enveloped in light, elongates like an image in a funhouse mirror and then disappears with a sound best described as "poit!"

He laughs and mumbles to himself: "Took you long enough! Ohhh, your mother was MUCH better at riding light beams than you."

A cat walks in the room, jumps up on the table and plops down on the open book.

"Nicodemus! I was reading that!"

The cat turns over to be better exposed to the sunlight.

"No matter, I suppose I had better go to the river to see if she got there alright."

The cat yawns and utters a meow.

The old man shakes his head and grabs his staff.

"Yes, Nicodemus. I'll bring back dinner!"

The old man mumbles something, the top hat like symbol on his staff glows brilliant yellow and he, too is gone.

Miles mean nothing in this place, if it is a place.

However in a blink of an eye he is there at the river's edge. He hears a sloshing sound coming up from behind him. He turns around and sees a dripping wet Cassiopeia walking up to him.

"Guess I was visualizing the river a little too much!"

The old man snaps his fingers and a towel appears.

"Thanks gramps."

Cassiopeia dries herself off.

The old man smiles: "You look a lot like your mother."

"She didn't have all these freckles, did she?"

"Oh yes, she did. Family trait!"

"I hate them! How did she get rid of them? Magic??"

"No child, makeup!"

Cassiopeia brushes her long brown hair and then drops the brush and rushes to river's edge:

"Grandfather! I hear them!!"

A low hum can be heard from downstream. The hum gets louder and louder.

Soon hundreds of the creatures looking just like that one in the old man's house rush past, swimming upstream.

"Can I catch some songs, gramps?"

"Just one, Cassiopeia. We always have to maintain the balance."

Cassiopeia tries to catch one with her bare hands, slips on the rocks and falls once again in to the river!

She pulls herself out as the old man conjures up two more towels.

"Cassiopeia, how about we just sit for a while?"

"I'm all for that gramps."

They walk over to a bench and sit down.

Cassiopeia brushes her hair once again; "Is this where mom first brought dad?"

The old man looks around: "Yes, I think so."

"They fell in love here?"

"No, love takes time."

"She never told me about this place, or about you."

"That's because I had to make her forget."

"Why?!"

"It's a long story."

"But they did meet here?"

"No, they met in school."

"Well, if she doesn't remember all this can you tell me how they met?"

The old man looked around as if remembering; he smiled as a tear came to his eye: "Sure."

"Cool!"

The old man snapped his fingers and a blanket appeared.

Cassiopeia laughed: "No, I meant that it would be great to hear about it!"

The both laughed and Cassiopeia wrapped herself up in the blanket.

The old man looked around and saw the gate in the distance: Well they came through that gate, but how they got to that gate and what happened afterwards, now that's the story…"

Eastern High School 1974

"...That was "Aquarius/Let the Sunshine In" by The 5th Dimension..."

The radio faded as Keith Newheart walked away from the car and towards the building. Keith, wearing his army style shirt and Levi's.

He couldn't wait until he could drive. That Ford Galaxy his friend's brother drove was HUGE. They could actually GO places! It was still a year off so he had to deal with walking to school.

He walked up the stairs and noticed this girl he had never seen before standing near the door. Her long strawberry blonde hair blew in the gentle breeze. She looked lost. Keith, being Keith, looked away afraid she might notice his stare.

He continued on past her and in to the halls of Eastern High School. The girl turned and looked back to him. She was holding a medallion with a funny top hat like symbol on it in her left hand. She smiled, laughed, shook her head and held out her right hand into the sunlight. Everything looked golden for a moment and she wasn't there anymore.

Keith's first class was history. He loved the class, not the teacher, Mr. Studerbaker. The teacher talked in a low monotone and made things seem as exciting as watching the grass grow. Keith, however, loved history. He would visualize in his head the events as they happened, almost putting himself there in the story, the action.

Keith walked in and sat in his seat just as the late bell sounded. He noticed that Mr. Clayborn was at Mr. Studerbaker 's desk. Mr. Clayborn looked up and called attendance. Afterwards he stood at the chalkboard and told the class that:

"Mr. Studerbaker won't be here today..."

Of course he was drowned out by a shout of approval. He shook his head:

"As I <u>was</u> saying, Mr. Studerbaker won't be in today. Before I go any further, I want you all to welcome a new student here at Eastern. Everybody say a big hello to...uh..DE-LINE-NI Wilson. Is that the right way to pronounce your name?"

The same girl Keith saw at the door stood up in the middle of the room:

"Yes Mr. Clayborn, Delineni, you got it right."

Keith already had noticed that there was something strange about her but he could not put his finger on it.

Mr. Clayborn looked at her:

"Interesting name, Delineni, some day you must tell us what, if anything it means."

Without letting her respond he changed subjects and continued:

"Ok, now Mr. Studerbaker wants you all to watch President Nixon's address tonight and write an essay on it."

The class moaned.

The class dragged on for Keith. Now and then he glanced over to this Delineni girl. She seemed distracted. She kept looking at this medallion that was in her hand. Delineni turned to look him right in the eyes. She smiled and Keith looked down towards his book, which he hit with his hand and knocked to the floor with a "slap!"

Mr. Clayborn looked over to Keith:

"Troubles, Keith?"

Someone yelled out: "The dork dropped his book!"

Keith just picked up the book and looked down at the desk.

Mr. Clayborn continued on with his lecture…
Several classes later it was finally lunch period.

Keith got food from the line and went to sit at the same table in the corner where he always sat. There were a couple of guys sitting at the other end of the table. No one said a thing to Keith.

A few moments later one of those guys whistled:

"Look at the new girl!"

They became totally silent as she walked past them and sat next to Keith.

Of course this was something that Keith wasn't accustomed to so he just looked at his food and kept eating.

Delineni played with her mashed potatoes:

"What is this stuff?"

Keith looked up:

"Um, mashed potatoes, gravy and meatloaf!"

"You have such funny food here!"

Keith laughed:

"There's nothing funny about meatloaf!"

Delineni took a bite of the meatloaf, made a face, and laughed.

Keith felt at ease, something he did not usually feel. So he started talking:

 "You are new around here aren't you?"

"Yes I am..."

A very strange look came to her face.

"...I've come a great non-distance to be here in this place!"

"A non-distance?"

"Yeah, but we'll talk more about that later, ok Keith?"

She said that with a smile, but still with this odd look on her face. The way she said it was almost in awe!

"Well..um, ok."

The bell sounded and she got up to go. Keith looked at her, shook his head:

"Hey, how do you know my name?"

"Oh, dad told me."

"Your dad told you my name?"

"Yeah, oh there's the second bell we gotta go."

"Who's your dad?"

She just walked away: "See ya later, Keith!"

"..From 1969 that was the Neon Philharmonic and "Morning Girl..."

It was pouring rain as Keith ran past the cars and into the school. It had been a month since he met Delineni.

Delineni had continued to sit with Keith during lunch, much to the amazement of both Keith and the other students. They would talk about class, music, art and writing. Delineni loved to draw and Keith loved to write, mostly poetry.

Delineni had sketched a picture from one of his poems. A snow scene with wolf tracks leading towards a full moon. It was then that Keith noticed that she drew a lot of mythical creatures. They all looked different, but she also drew a lot of wizards. They were different poses of the same wizard. He always meant to ask her about the wizard and the funny top hat like symbol that was always drawn along with him, but Keith always got distracted and forgot.

Keith still considered Delineni a little weird, but it was nice to have a friend, not to mention the fact that she was a very beautiful friend! Keith liked being the center of attention for once.

Jay Martin, from stage crew, began to tease Keith about her. Jay was nice, Keith would sit with him at lunch if they had the same lunch period, but they didn't.

Of course, stage crew was the place Keith enjoyed the most. He could run the lights, the audio, or sometimes the projector. It was kind of cool to do all that stuff behind the scenes of a show and have it all go well!

Keith was at school late that day due to a rehearsal for the talent show. It was <u>still</u> pouring rain when he left. Keith was running home, his coat over his thick hair. He heard footsteps behind him so he turned around to see Delineni running behind him. Keith stopped.

She made a short dash and came up next to him and smiled:

"Hi."

Keith smiled: "Hi, what are you doing at school so late?"

"I'm trying out for cheerleading."

"Cool!, did you make it?"

"Don't know yet."

Keith nodded his head: "It's really raining! I live about two blocks down the street. Where do you live?"

Delineni's long hair was drenched and she looked to be shivering:

"About a block down in the old yellow brick house."

"You're kidding?!"

"Nope."

"Delineni, that house is about a block away from mine, we're neighbors!!

She smiled: "I know, I just moved in a week before we met."

"Wow, that house had been deserted for years. Everyone always says that it's supposed to be haunted!"

"People only say that 'cause they don't understand."

Keith looked puzzled:

"What's there to understand?"

Delineni got the same very strange look on her face as the day they met.

"Hey, Dad's home, want to meet him?"

"Um, ok."

They walked up the steps of the old house. Keith smiled:

"I used to play here, Mom would always come and grab me before I could get in the door, though."

Delineni said softly: "That's because it wasn't the right time yet, Keith."

"Delineni, you're kind of creeping me out."

She smiled as they walked in the dilapidated house. There were cobwebs all around. Sheets over furniture, dust all everywhere. There were no signs that anyone had lived there for years.

"Delineni! You live here?"

She took that medallion out of her pocket.

"Not exactly!"

Keith got very creeped out: "I think I should go home."

"Awww, don't go yet! I promised dad he could meet you!"

"Delineni, no one has lived here for <u>years</u>!"

"Have you ever read "Alice in Wonderland" Keith?"

"Huh? Yeah when I was a kid. What's that got to do with this?"

"Well, Lewis Carroll almost got it right! Trust me Keith."

The top hat like symbol on her medallion glowed with golden light as Delineni took Keith's hand in hers and they walked up to a huge mirror.

"Keith, would you like to meet my Dad and have a little adventure to write about?"

"Um, will I be home for dinner?"

"I think we can manage that!"

"Ok"

Delineni pulled Keith forward, the medallion glowing brilliant gold and they walked through the mirror...

<u>Wonder</u>

One moment they were in an old, dilapidated, house during a rainstorm. The next moment they were walking out of what looked to be a huge mirror at the top of a hill.

The sun was warm, the sun was bright. Birds sang and butterflies flew.

Keith spun around, looking everywhere, mouth open:

"We were... and now we are... Where? Where are we Delineni?"

Delineni laughed:

"My home, Keith."

"You live here? On this hill?"

"No, I live in a house near the river's edge."

She pointed down and Keith saw a shimmering river and next to it a thatch roofed house, smoke coming from its chimney.

Keith guessed that it was about 3 miles away and nodded:

"What do you call this place?"

Delineni smiled:

"This is the land of Wonder, Keith."

"The land of Wonder?"

"Yeah, this is the place built by everyone's dreams, wishes and hopes! This place is built by awe and wonder, by love of word and rhyme, paint and brush, dance, and music, oh….music!"

As she said this she was glowing, Keith thought. Glowing with love, glowing with some kind of steadfast esteem. This was her home and she loved it with all her heart.

Delineni took Keith's hand in hers:

"Lets go."

The walked down the hill and towards the house.

It wasn't much longer until Keith started to hear music.

"Delineni I hear a song. Do you?"

"There are lots of songs here, Keith! We are still a ways from the river so I think we are listening to Pan.

"The Greek God?"

"Uh huh, he likes to hang out here and play his flute when he is sad."

"Sad?"

"He almost *always* is, you know!"

"Why?"

"Well…"

Delineni was interrupted by a deep booming voice:

"Hush, child! You are disturbing my piping!"

Delineni jumped and looked to the side at the same time Keith did. They both looked up to see Pan standing there his flute in one hand and a **very** large frown on his face.

"Oh! I'm sorry Pan! I didn't realize that we were so close to you."

"Well, it's too late now. You've interrupted a perfectly good lament!"

Keith spoke up:

"What do you have to be sad about?"

Pan turned violently around and almost charged Keith.

"You think my life is all milk and honey, eh?"

"Well, you <u>are</u> a Greek God, sir!"

"I am, am I? Tell that to the Nymphs! They harass me morning, noon and night!

"They do?"

Just then they all heard a high-pitched laugh, a giggle and the rustle of branches like someone or some thing moved through them.

"There's one now! Come here my dear Nymph! Just one kiss, my dear…"

With that Pan took off after the Nymph. As he charged away we heard that high-pitched giggle now and then. Slowly fading away as she lead Pan on yet another wild goose chase.

Delineni was laughing very hard:

"Don't worry, Keith. He'll soon be back playing his sad lament!"

"How many times does he do this?"

Delineni shook her head:

"How many times does the sun set?"

Keith shrugged and they both laughed.

A hummingbird flew up to Keith and Delineni. Its wings sang a tune, in beat with the upstroke.

"Delineni, Delineni, sweet *child of light.* Your father calls!"

Delineni curtsied to the hummingbird and turned to Keith:

"We're late; I have to grab a light beam so we can get home quickly."

"What?!"

"Do you believe in me?"

"Sure, I guess."

"No guessing! Do you believe in me, do you believe that this is all real?"

Keith looked in to her eyes:

"Yes, Delineni. I believe in you."

She gave Keith a hug while reaching out with one hand to the sunlight. Her hand touched the sunlight and began to move <u>into</u> it, *blurring* and becoming longer. Keith and Delineni became enveloped in light, they elongated like an image in a funhouse mirror. Keith blinked his eyes and the hill was gone and they were standing on the banks of a river.

"About time you showed up young lady!"

The voice came from a man standing several feet in front of them. The man was holding a wooden staff with a golden symbol on the top. The symbol looked like the one on Delineni's medallion.

"I came as soon as Sam told me!"

Keith laughed:

"The hummingbird's name is Sam?!"

Delineni shook her head:

"Oh no, Sam is short for his real name."

Oh, what's his real name?

"Why, Samuel, of course!"

Keith sighed…

"Uh Hum!"

Delineni blushed:

"Oh! I'm sorry, Dad, this is Keith. Keith, this is my father, Taslasness.

Keith moved to shake the wizard's hand but Taslasness was talking:

"Keith? Keith?! No, that won't do, that won't do at all."

Keith was now very confused:

"Pardon me, sir?"

"What do you seek, Keith?"

"Um, my dinner?"

Delineni laughed.

Taslasness shushed her and turned back to Keith:

"Keith, what do you seek? What do you wish to learn?"

"I don't know! I just want to fit in, not be such a dork all the time."

Taslasness turned to Delineni: "What is this word, Dork?"

"It means he feels clumsy, unsure of himself, ugly."

Delineni winced as she said the words, as if the voicing of them hurt her.

"Ahh, I see!"

The wizard pointed his staff at the river, which immediately stopped flowing:

"Do you know the story of the ugly duckling?"

"Yeah, what does that have to do with any of this?"

"You are not what you <u>will</u> be! Life will shape you and like that ugly duck you will find that you are so much more!"

The wizard adjusted his pointed hat and swirled his staff in the river water which started to boil, turn into a mist:

"Keith, you say, Keith…"

Keith's name is now spelled in the rising mist, the letters floating in the air.

Now the mist takes the shape of a swan. The letters fading out in to the swan's white feathers.

"Pay attention for a name is an important thing! Here to and now, I name you.

- **K** is for *Keith*
- **A** is for *always remember us*
- The **Swan** is for *what you shall become!*

Your name, your <u>given</u> name here in the Land of Wonder is Kaswan! Share it only with those you love, use it to call magick high, remember it when you wish to return here."

Delineni walked to Keith, kissed him on the cheek:

"Welcome to the Land of Wonder, Kaswan!"

Taslasness smiled:

"These are your first footsteps into a new life, Kaswan."

"I don't feel any different."

"Change takes time, Kaswan. Look back at this day 10, 20, 30 years hence and you might not even recognize yourself!"

Kaswan looked at the funny top hat symbol on the wizard's staff. Taslasness caught his eye:

"No more questions for now. It's dinner you want and it's dinner you'll get!"

A flash and they were all gathered 'round an alabaster table loaded with a feast.

Kaswan looked at it all and then back to the wizard:

"But my family's going to start missing me soon!"

Delineni smiled:

"Time runs slower in your reality, only half a minute has passed since we left."

"Really?"

Taslasness shook his head:

"Is he always so disbelieving?"

Delineni smiled:

"Father Look at what I brought. It's a delicacy from Kaswan's reality. It's called meatloaf and mashed potatoes…"

Triad

Kaswan blinked his eyes and opened them. Golden sunshine was on his face, the sound of a teapot on the boil was down the hall and he was in an unfamiliar bed.

He looked around the room, saw no one and got out of the bed. He found that, save for his shoes, he was still fully dressed.

"Good morning!"

Kaswan turned his head and saw Delineni walking in the room carrying a tray with a teapot and what looked to be large cookies on it.

"Delineni, what happened? Last thing I remember we were eating then I woke up?"

She laughed:

"You fell asleep in your mashed potatoes! Moving through the gateway between realities takes a lot out of you."

"But I felt fine!"

"'Cause you were excited, then you calmed down and, well, you re-mashed the potatoes!"

"What are those?"

"Tea and scones."

"Scones?"

"Kind of like a sweet biscuit with raisins. Tastes good with butter."

Kaswan took a bite and smiled.

Delineni pointed at his shoes on the floor;

"Dad wants to see us after we eat."

"Oh? Where is he?"

"He's at the River of Life."

"River of Life?"

"Uh, huh – He has to catch today's crop of new songs."

"Huh?!"

"He'll explain when we see him, more tea?"

Breakfast done, Kaswan and Delineni walked the short distance from the house to the river.

"Hey, Delineni?"

She stopped walking and turned around.

"Delineni, what kind of flower is this?"

"It's a Mood Orchid."

"I've never seen a flower change colors!"

"You know mood rings, right?"

"Yeah, they change color according to your mood."

"The Mood Orchid reflects your mood back at you so you can see it, look:"

She stepped in front of the flower and it changed from blue to green;

See?

"Cool!"

She picked the flower and handed it to Kaswan;

"Now you will always know what mood you are in!"

Delineni laughed as Kaswan put the flower in his pants pocket.

As they continued to walk to the river Kaswan heard what could only be described as several songs being played at once with water gurgling interspersed between the notes.

"Is Pan back?"

Delineni smiled and started to run;

"Oh, I want to hear today's catch, come on!"

Kaswan took off after her;

"Hear today's catch?"

She laughed as they burst out of the trees and to the River's bank. There standing at the same place they met yesterday was Taslasness. He was holding a net which was filled with what looked like fishes except with each wiggle music came from them.

One fish was struggling to get out of the net more then the rest. With each move came an ear crushing burst of sound.

Delineni laughed;

"You caught a heavy metal one there Dad!"

The wizard sighed;

"No kidding! Help me get these into the well, child!"

Kaswan stood, dumbfounded

They walked over to what looked like a transparent water well. It shimmered much like the mirror they walked through on the journey here.

They then carefully poured the fish-things in to the well, each disappearing in a small golden flash of light. The heavy metal one was the last to go.

Taslasness smiled;

"I like peace and quiet!"

Delineni shook her head;

"You're boring!"

"I'm ages old, child, of course I'm boring!"

She gave him a hug and then in unison they both looked to Kaswan still standing there dumbfounded.

"What just happened?"

"Dad harvested the latest crop of songs from the River of Life and sent them to Earth."

"What?!"

Taslasness nodded in agreement with Delineni:

"We send them to Earth, and then someone writes them, makes them real."

"But they're fishes. How can someone write a fish?"

Delineni smiled;

"They're idea fishes. Dad handles the ones for music."

"Idea fishes?"

"They swim into someone's consciousness and give them an idea. They are drawn to the person that needs them the most. In this case they will swim to someone writing a song."

Taslasness laughed;

"If heavy metal **is** a song, that is!"

"Dad!"

Kaswan sat down on a rock;

"You called this the River of Life?"

Taslasness shook his head:

"You are on the banks of the River of Life. This is the one river that joins all humanity together. Connected together through song, ideas, creativity, worship, love and everything in between.

The river is more. It supplies water for the great tree, its roots which form the fabric of space time and everything that was, is, <u>will</u> be."

Kaswan turned pale:

"How? How does it do these things?"

"Have you ever heard of a man named Albert Einstein?"

"Yeah, in school. He was a great physicist. But what does he have to do with this stuff?"

"A great deal, Kaswan. Do you see this symbol?"

Taslasness held up is staff and showed the top hat like symbol to Kaswan.

"Yeah, Delineni has something like it to."

"Indeed she does. This is called the Triad. It is based on science, love, and magick."

"What does this have to do with Einstein?"

"It's not only Einstein, but others like him."

"Ok, so what does it all mean?"

"Energy and matter are the same thing."

"Huh?"

"Stomp your foot."

"Ok..."

Kaswan stomped is foot on the ground.

"Did you feel the ground while you stomped on it?"

"Sure!"

"Did you know that it's not real, that it is only energy whose current form is the ground?"

"But it's ground, solid Earth!"

"Nothing is solid, here or anywhere."

Delineni jumped back as Taslasness waved his staff: the ground turned to water, Kaswan falling in, up to his head

"Hey!"

Another wave of the wizard's staff and Kaswan was floating above the water which, in turn, changed back to "solid" ground.

Delineni tried very hard not to laugh as Taslasness waved his staff one last time. This time Kaswan dropped back to the ground as a large towel materialized above Kaswan and dropped on his head.

"Very funny!"

This time Delineni did laugh.

Taslasness smiled:

"Nothing is solid, because nothing is real. It's all made up of energy which has a current illusionary form. E=mc2"

Kaswan dried himself off:

"That's what they said in class."

"Right, energy is matter and matter is energy."

"Is that how you change things?"

Taslasness smiled:

"Partially: That and hundreds of years of practice."

"So _everything_ is energy?"

"Yes."

"What does that have to do with what you asked me when I got here?"

"You mean about you feeling like a dork and all?"

Kaswan threw the towel back the wizard:

"Yeah."

"Because feelings, emotions, even love, itself are forms of energy."

"Really?"

"And being energy, they are eternal, as are you."

"I'm not eternal!"

"True enough, you will eventually die. But the energy that is you: your, for lack of a better word, soul will continue."

"Like what they teach in church?"

"There are many different beliefs, Kaswan. They are all right and they are all wrong. You are not here to get religion, do that elsewhere. I simply state the facts."

"Love is forever?"

"If it's real and not some infatuation, yes."

"What's the difference?"

"Biology."

"Huh?"

"Infatuation, lust, are things that do not last. While they are real, in their own right, they are not love. The energy of these emotions will soon transmute to another, usually boredom!"

"Transmute?"

"Change. Again, energy never ends, it just changes form."

"So what makes love different? Why doesn't it change to something else?"

Taslasness smiled;

"Because it does change, Kaswan. It changes to itself."

Kaswan sat down, his still wet clothes flopping in to the grass;

"I think I'm getting a headache!"

"Good! That means you are thinking this out for yourself."

"How can love change back into itself?"

"Because true love *is* change, Kaswan. It never stays the same! It is passion, it is commitment, it is mother, father, child, God and then back again. True love is never, ever the same."

Kaswan shrugged: "I can't understand this."

"Yes you can, Keith."

Delineni looked surprised that her father used Kaswan's other name but she said nothing.

Kaswan nodded his head;

"I think I have a lot to think about!"

Taslasness laughed:

"Thought is the pathway to knowledge!"

Kaswan looked at the wizard's staff;

"So, you still haven't explained the Triad."

Taslasness nodded:

"Does it look a little familiar to you?"

Kaswan nodded;

"Yes, yes it does!"

"Science and magick, Kaswan."

Kaswan smiled, he smiled and laughed;

"It's a modified Pi symbol, isn't it?"

"Yes it is Kaswan."

"Why?"

"Because using Pi and the many formulae derived from it you can learn about much of the universe!"

"But it isn't Pi, it's different."

"We use it to represent universal love."

"Oh, no. Not more about that!"

Taslasness looked at Kaswan. He appeared to look almost angry until he sat down on a log and started to laugh very hard.

"Yes, a little more. Then I'll finish – for now."

Kaswan just sighed.

"Do you see that there are numbers to the left, right, and top of the symbol?"

"Yes; the number 1 is on the left, the number 2 is on the right and the number 3 is on the raised portion in the middle. The top of the top hat, I guess."

"What else do you see?"

"Well, there's a sidewise number eight under the whole symbol."

"That is the symbol for infinity, Kaswan."

"Like, forever?"

"Yes, forever."

Ok, so what does it all mean?"

Taslasness's eyes glowed golden for a moment then he smiled;

"The numbers 1 and 2 are alone, separated. But when they join, to form the three they become love which is elevated above them all. Love which always changes but never ends. The three is infinity, the three is forever."

"So they, the 1 and 2 can be people?"

"People, ideas, animals, the entire sum of creation and beyond!"

"My headache is coming back!"

"I think we have given you a lot to think about, Kaswan! Best to end the lesson now."

"But! I don't want to go!"

Delineni took Kaswan's hand;

"Don't worry, you'll be back!"

"I will?"

"Sure, as many times as you want."

"How do I get back here?"

Delineni let go of Kaswan's hand. He still felt something in his hand and looked down to it. There was a medallion like Delineni's in his hand. It was pulsing a dim gold.

"Take this and when you feel the need to return here hold it to your heart."

"That's it?"

Taslasness laughed;

"For now Keith, for now!"

Delineni took his hand again;

"I'll walk you to the gate."

They walked through the field and back up the hill to the gate. They stopped in front of it.

Kaswan looked at Delineni;

"Will you be back at school?"

"Nope, I was never there."

"Huh?"

She kissed him on the cheek and everything turned black.

"…That was "Changes" by "David Bowie.""

Keith was up out of bed like a bolt. He turned off the alarm radio, looked around the room and considered the weird dream he just had.

"Keith! Get up! You <u>are</u> late for school!"

It was his step mother.

He threw on the pants he wore yesterday, a clean shirt and he was out the door.

Keith ran to school and was just in time for the last bell.

He was so tired, like he hadn't slept for days. In study hall, which was held in the school auditorium he actually nodded off before the aid yelled at him.

Jay was sitting next to him and laughed;

"Were you up all night or something?"

"Feels like it…"

Keith drifted off, but not to sleep. He was looking at the door. Jay looked too and they both smiled.

A girl neither one of them had ever seen before walked in and was asking the aid if she was in the right place. They heard her say that her name was Cindy.

Jay nudged Keith:

"Hey, you got a pencil. I want to sketch her."

"Sure."

Keith looked in his pocket for the pencil and instead pulled out a glowing flower.

"Keith, what is that?"

Keith looked at the glowing Mood Orchard in amazement;

"It wasn't a dream?!!"

"What wasn't?"

But Keith wasn't listening to Jay. The new girl, Cindy had just walked past and sat in the row across from them. Keith looked, briefly to the Mood Orchard and saw it change to a deep red.

Keith smiled and thought to himself: "Don't need no stupid flower to tell me that…"

Epilog

The old wizard had fallen asleep in mid sentence. He was sitting atop an old tree stump. His long beard gently moving back and forth with each loud snore.

Cassiopeia took the blanket off, wrapped it around him and started to walk away.

"What? No questions Cassiopeia? That's not like you."

"I thought you were asleep."

"I was, now I'm not."

Taslasness pulled the blanket closer to him and looked to the girl for her first question.

"Okay, who was that Cindy girl?"

"She was his first love."

"Aw! Wait, you mean Mom wasn't his first love?!"

"No, she was years later. Remember Cassiopeia, love takes time."

"Where is she now?"

"Cindy died a few months before your Father graduated."

"She died?!"

"Yes, she drove off a bridge and in to the Chicago river."

"Wow, I never knew."

"Your father never talks about it."

"Does he remember?"

Taslasness almost winced;

"Yes, he will <u>always</u> remember that."

They were silent for a while, Cassiopeia kicking stones in to the river.

"Careful, Cassiopeia, you don't want to hit an idea fish."

She smiled;

"Are you going to teach me all that complicated stuff about love and physics?"

"There's nothing complicated about it."

"Grandfather, **I** was getting a headache just listening to you!"

The old wizard walked up to Cassiopeia and kissed her on the forehead.

She giggled;

"What's _that_ for?"

"It's for all the wonderful headaches to come!"

Cassiopeia rolled her eyes as they started to walk back towards the house, Nicodemus's meows for dinner already audible.

FIN!!!

Other Works in This Series

- H.S. 1974, Awakings - Audio play, June 1974, 110 Minutes.
- The Mystery of <u>HIM</u> - Stage Play, 1975.
- The Trilogy - Short Story, 1982
- Magic - Short Story, April 1992
- The Poets Corner - March and April 1994 issues.
- Trilogy's End – Short Story, 1995
- Trilogy's End – Stage Play, 1996

Who Is Kevin James Keyser?

Kevin has been writing since the early 1970's.

Kevin is the founder of the Amateur Recording Association (ARA) of Chicago an entertainment group that produced plays, audio plays, and films in the period between 1974 and 1986.

Kevin published "The Poets Corner", a monthly poetry newsletter, from 1987 - 1999. The Poets Corner is widely credited with being the first non-technical e-zine to arise during the infancy of BBSing and the Internet.

Kevin published "The Write Time", a regular newsletter about the written and spoken word from 1999 - 2000.

Kevin is a performance poet, performing on stage at a variety of spoken word venues including two performances at the Chicago Cultural Center.

Kevin has hosted poetry readings at:
- The Sun Cafe (Regular Host)
- No Exit Cafe (Guest Host)
- Cafe Aloha (Guest Host)

Television appearances:
- Songsation (1998)
- Strictline (2000)

Radio appearances:

- David Rubin, Cafe Aloha on WZRD (1998)
- Wordslingers On WLUW (2000)

Films include:

- "Search'n": A film short. "Search'n took everyday scenes and placed them to music. Shot on glorious super 8mm film and synchronized to a cassette audio track. (1977)
- "A Touch of Magic" Experimental animation storyboard. The adventures of Juniper the elf as she helps Santa bring Christmas Joy. (1978)

Videos include:

- The Final Chop: Experimental computer animation. We follow the exploits of Horance the Turkey a day before Thanksgiving. (198?)

Original Audio plays Include:

- E.D. In the year of 1973 (Pilot to The H.S. Series)
- The H.S. series (1974 –1977)
- Lonely Is The Hunter (1978)
- The Minstrel Man (1978)
- H.S. - The Metamorphosis (1979)
- The Co Ho Show (1977 – 1979)
- Radio WCLD (A.K.A. Jane Byrne and the Salt Truck Triumph!) (1979)
- Move'n On! (1979 – 1980)

Short Stories Include:

- The Trilogy (1982)
- Specter (1991)
- Trilogy's End (1995)
- Questing The Prize (1999)
- Awakings (2009)
- The Mystery of Him (2014)

Novella's Include:

- Love - The Many Eyed Beast (1988)
- A Twinkle in God's Eye (2006)

Plays Include:

- The Anatomy Of A Disk Jockey (1976)
- The Mystery of Him (1977)
- Trilogy's End (1997)

Audio Productions Include:

- H.S. The Special Tapes (1977)
- Moments of Life (198?)
- Questing The Prize (2000)
- The River - Spoken Word on CD (2002)

Current Projects:

- The Amazingly Annoying Life of Kevin Keyser – Memoir
- Poets Corner 2 – Quarterly (mostly)

Future Projects:

- Web Of Eye's – A Short Story
- The Golden Corpuscle - A Novel